For Sinbad and Holly, the inspiration
for the ship's cat, and without whose
interruptions we would have got this
story finished in half the time

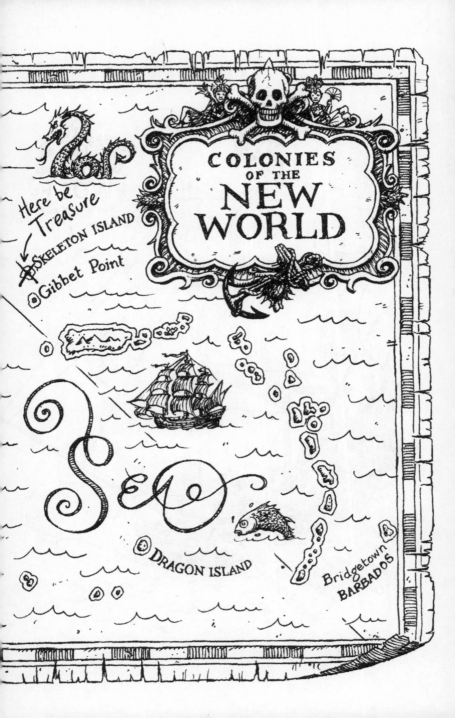

The SEA WOLF

Captain's Cabin
Hammocks
Gun Deck
Galley
Ship's Stores

CHAPTER ONE

Sam Silver raced up the high street of Backwater Bay and skidded through the door of his parents' fish and chip shop.

"I'm home!" he yelled as he sped past his mother and up to their flat on the first floor. He was too busy to stop and chat. He was on a mission. It had been a long hard day of spellings and maths at school and he'd promised himself an exciting pirate adventure to help him recover.

His friends had exciting pirate adventures by reading about them in books or playing computer games, but Sam had an amazing secret. He'd found a magic coin that could whisk him off to join Captain Blade's crew on board the *Sea Wolf*, a pirate ship from over three hundred years ago. And the great thing was that when he was back in 1706, looking for treasure and fighting sea battles, not one second went by in the present – so no one missed him.

Since his mum would definitely notice if he got his school uniform blown up by cannonballs or nibbled by sharks, Sam always wore an old T-shirt and jeans on his time travels. He pulled his drawer open to find them and stopped in horror. Normally they were crumpled up at the back behind his socks. Today they were lying neatly folded right on top. And – which was worse – they'd been washed and ironed!

Sam had a horrible sinking feeling as if someone had pulled a plug in his tummy. It would be bad enough wearing clean clothes on a pirate ship, but he'd suddenly remembered that he'd left his magic doubloon in his jeans. He'd taken the coin from the bottle on his shelf to set off on an adventure last night when his mum had appeared at his bedroom door. He'd quickly shoved the coin into his pocket and that's where it was now. At least, he hoped so. Suppose it had been washed out of his jeans and into the water to disappear for ever down the drain?

Frantically he searched, turning his trousers inside-out and shaking them hard. Nothing. He was never going to see his buccaneer friends again.

Then he realised he'd missed the tiny
pocket under the waistband. He pushed
two fingers in — it was empty. The washing
machine had eaten his precious coin! Wait
a minute. What about the time he'd left
a football medal among his clothes? His
mum had found it in the rubber bit round
the door of the machine. Maybe that's
where the doubloon would be! But as
Sam raced into the kitchen he nearly fell
over a man in overalls who was taking the
washing machine apart.

Sam's face fell.

"It looks bad, doesn't it?" said the man cheerily. "This pipe's jammed. There's something stuck in it."

"What is it?" asked Sam.

"Not sure," said the man. "It's hard to tell with all the muck in there." He fed a rod down the pipe.

Sam held his breath. The man pulled out a lump of sludge and poked about in it. "Got it!" he said at last, holding up a dirty metal disc. "It's a coin — bit funny looking, though." He went to give it a wipe with a cloth.

"No!" cried Sam, scared that if the man rubbed it he'd be the one to disappear back to 1706. "It's mine," he added quickly. "Thanks. I'll take it."

Sam ran back to his room. He had to find out if his gold doubloon still worked. It wasn't meant to go through the wash! Its special power had probably been flushed away. He pulled on his horribly neat T-shirt and jeans. Then he spat on the coin and gave it a rub.

At once he was whooshed up inside a dark, spinning tunnel.

He'd been silly to think that the washing machine could have destroyed the magic. The coin just needed a bit of Silver spit and polish.

"*Sea Wolf*, here I come!" he yelled.

In an instant Sam found himself sprawled across the floor of a small room, surrounded by wooden barrels and coils of rope. Awesome! He was back in the storeroom on the *Sea Wolf*. The ship was swaying beneath his feet as he put on his jerkin, neckerchief and belt and picked up his spyglass. His friend Charlie always made sure they were left there for him. Charlie was the only member of the crew who knew he came from the twenty-first century. The others believed that each time he disappeared, he had just dashed off home to help his poor widowed mum on her farm. None of his shipmates thought this was odd, as pirates love their mothers more than anything else.

Sam stowed the coin safely in his pocket. Then he ran out of the storeroom and made for the deck, taking the steps in three bounds. The crew were busy splicing ropes, mending sails and climbing the rigging. They sang a cheerful sea shanty as they worked in the hot Caribbean sunshine. Sam could see Charlie helping Ned the bosun mend a broken piece of

the starboard rail. Ned swung his hammer
in time to the song, joining in the chorus
with a booming voice.

Captain Blade stood close by, peering at
a map. He was pulling at the braids in his
beard, deep in thought.

"Head south, shipmates," he ordered. "I
warrant the French treasure galleons will
be coming that way."

"Aye!" cried a stubbly-faced man with a
wooden leg. He turned the ship's wheel to
set the course. "And with this fair wind,

we'll be meeting them before midday or my name's not Harry Hopp!"

Excellent! thought Sam. *I've got back just in time for a treasure hunt.*

"Mainsail all correct, Captain," came a cry from above his head and Fernando shot down the rigging, his hands and feet moving so fast they were a blur. "Do you want me on lookout now?"

"No need for that," called Sam, running to the middle of the deck. "*I'm* here and ready for duty in the crow's nest."

Fernando let out a Spanish exclamation and slapped Sam hard on the back, a huge grin on his face at the sight of his friend.

"Sam Silver!" declared the captain. "By Jupiter's chariot, how did you get to us a day's sail from land? You couldn't have swum that far!"

Sam was always so excited at being back on the *Sea Wolf* that he never remembered to think up how he might have got there.

If he said that he'd popped back from three hundred years in the future they'd think he'd lost his wits.

"He must have climbed aboard at Tortuga when we stopped for provisions," said Charlie, coming to his rescue as usual.

"That's right," said Sam, gratefully.

"We never saw you," said Harry Hopp, frowning.

"That's because . . ." Sam began, thinking furiously.

"That's because he was asleep in the hold," said Charlie. "He was snoring like a warthog. I'm surprised you didn't hear him!"

"I was exhausted by the time I got here," added Sam. "My mum wanted me to muck out the pigs and milk the goat before I left."

"What a dutiful son," said Harry.

"Your poor mother," added Ned the

bosun, wiping away a tear.
"Managing a whole farm
on her own."

"Well, I'm very
grateful she could
spare you," said
Captain Blade.
"Get up into that
crow's nest, lad. We
need you to keep a weather eye out for the
French ships laden with treasure!"

Sam didn't need telling twice. "Aye, aye,
Captain!" he cried happily.

CHAPTER TWO

Sam had just started climbing the rigging when there was a flutter of green feathers and a parrot landed on the rope in front of him. It began chewing at the nearest knot.

"Hello, Crow," said Sam in delight. "What are you up to?"

"Take that pesky bird aloft with you!" yelled Ned, waving his hammer. "He's been mad hungry these past few days, gnawing at anything he could find. I've had to replace two chair legs and half the ship's rail!"

"But not before I'd sat on the chair and gone tumbling!" growled Harry Hopp. "That varmint will be after my wooden leg next."

"Don't be too hard on him," said Peter the cook. "You know he's been ill. He didn't eat for a week."

"That's because you fed him your oyster stew," said Charlie.

Crow turned his head on one side and peered at Sam. Then he flew onto his shoulder and began to nibble at his leather jerkin.

"Poor thing," said Sam, stroking his crest. "I know what's wrong," he told the crew. "It's not that he's hungry. If he's been ill, his beak will have overgrown. Parrots' beaks grow all the time and they have to gnaw on wood and things to trim them. They don't gnaw when they feel unwell, so now Crow's got extra gnawing to do to get his beak back to normal."

"How do you know that?" asked Peter.

Oops, thought Sam. *I can't tell them I heard it on a school trip to the zoo.*

"My mum told me," he blustered. "She's got loads of parrots . . . on her farm."

Captain Blade shuddered. "Sounds like a terrible place."

The bold Captain Blade, who would fight ten men at one go, was scared stiff of parrots. Harry Hopp said it was because one of the feathered fiends had dive-bombed him in his crib, but all the pirates told a different tale about their leader's one fear.

Sam swung up the rigging, the parrot

gripping tightly to his shoulder. As he
climbed over the side of the crow's nest,
the parrot flapped onto the flagpole and
started attacking it with his beak. Sam
swept the horizon with his spyglass. On
the port side a few ships were sailing by in
the distance but none was flying the plain
white French flag.

Sam looked to starboard. A single vessel
seemed to be heading their way.

He checked the flag at the top of the
mast. As the wind caught it he could make
out a shark over a skull and crossbones.

"Pirate ship ahoy!" he yelled. "Dead
ahead."

"Let's see if they want to share their
booty with us, lads," cried Harry Hopp
eagerly. "Get ready to 'persuade' them."

"I recognise that ship," reported
Fernando. "It's the *Truro*."

But Sam had spotted something strange.

"What's happened to her?" he called

down. "The sails are flapping loose. There's no sign of life."

He heard the captain burst out laughing. "I think our crafty friends are trying to outwit us. They're pretending they've abandoned ship."

"And as soon as we get close they'll attack," warned Ned.

"Go carefully, men," ordered Harry. "We'll show them we're no fools."

The crew ran to man the cannon.

As they sailed closer to the ship, Sam saw that parts of the *Truro*'s hull had been smashed, the rigging was in shreds and the mizzen mast torn from the deck. "I don't think it's a trick!" he exclaimed. "Looks like she's had a fight and the men are gone."

"Shiver me timbers, the boy's right," agreed Harry in surprise. He shouted orders to the crew. "Go about and get alongside. There may still be some pickings for us."

The crew quickly tethered the two ships
together and laid a plank bridge between
them. Sam sped down the rigging and ran
to the captain. "Permission to go aboard
with the others, sir?" he asked.

Blade nodded. "Follow me," he
commanded. "Weapons at the ready. This
could still be a trick."

Ben Hudson, the quartermaster, threw
Sam a cutlass and Sam climbed onto one
of the planks after Blade. The sea churned
far below. Being so high reminded him of

Monkey World at Backwater Bay, where you climbed tall trees and went down incredibly long zip wires — except that there were no helmets and safety ropes here. In fact, there was nothing between him and the ocean! Sam felt his legs tingle with terror and excitement.

He leapt onto the deck of the *Truro*. Charlie, Fernando and Ned followed, with other crew members close behind.

"Well, knock me down with a conker!" declared Ned. "This is a strange mess."

Knives and cutlasses lay scattered all over the place. Ben put his hand on a cannon. "Stone cold," he said. "I'd bet all the treasure in Trinidad that this hasn't been fired."

"I agree," said Captain Blade. "It looks as if there's been a fight but where are the bodies? Go carefully, shipmates."

Moving cautiously forwards, Sam noticed a dark liquid spattered over the

boards and seeping into the wood. *Blood!*
he thought with horror. Then he realised it
was more black than red.

"Check this out," he told Charlie. They
bent down to inspect it. "I think it's ink."

"That's odd," she replied. "Why would
anyone spill ink in the middle of a battle?
It's not the time to be writing letters!"

A terrified cry filled the air as a man
leapt out from a hatch in the deck. Eyes
wild in his pale face, he rounded on them

all, waving a broken oar. "Get away from me! I'll fight . . ." he quavered, his words tailing off as he stared at them. "I'll fight," he repeated with a sob.

"Is he mad?" asked Fernando.

The captain put his pistol in his belt and held out his hands towards the gibbering man. "It's Jem Plunkett, isn't it?" he said. "Ship's carpenter?"

"Aye," gasped Jem, collapsing in front of them, his makeshift weapon clattering down beside him.

Blade gripped his shoulder. "What's been going on here?" he asked. "Where is everyone?"

"Gone," croaked Jem. He looked round at them, horror all over his face. "They were taken." He gulped hard. "They were plucked from the ship like ants."

"He *is* crazed," declared Ned.

"No, I swear it," said the *Truro* pirate, clutching at the captain's sleeve. "It rose out of the waves and ate them in front of my very eyes!"

"What did?" asked Charlie in a frightened whisper.

"A huge sea monster."

CHAPTER THREE

Sam's jaw dropped open in amazement. He'd had no idea that sea monsters existed three hundred years ago — sea monsters big enough to devour a pirate crew! Although it was terrible that Jem's shipmates had been eaten by such a beast, Sam couldn't help feeling a little curious. He'd love to see a sea monster — from a safe distance, of course. It would be like spotting the Loch Ness Monster or a T Rex!

But the rest of the *Sea Wolf* crew didn't sound quite so keen.

"We should get as far from here as possible," said Ned. "French treasure ships or not."

There was a chorus of 'ayes' from the men behind.

"The creature may have had a hankering for French food and eaten the treasure fleet too," said Ben, eyeing the waves nervously.

Captain Blade stood pulling at the braids in his beard as he studied Jem. "Take your time," he said, "and tell us exactly what happened."

Jem gulped. "Well, we were making for Jamaica with a fine haul of gold when the monster suddenly reared out of the ocean, its arms waving above us. It was like a giant octopus. Those wicked tentacles tore at the sails and, all the while, it spat its ghastly ink at us."

"Did you try and fight?" asked Blade.

Jem frowned. "We were too terrified.
That thing shook the ship from bows
to stern. Some men fell overboard and
some took to the small boats, but then it
grabbed them . . ." He stopped, his eyes
filling with horror. "A huge mouth opened
and they disappeared inside. They were
gobbled up."

"How did you survive?" breathed
Fernando. Like the others, he was hanging
on Jem's every word.

"I dived into the hold and hid in an

empty barrel, sure that at any moment the monster would take the ship with me in it," Jem went on in a hushed voice. "I heard thumps and crashes and I knew it was those horrible arms searching for me. Then it all went quiet but I didn't dare venture out. I thought it must be lying in wait still. I don't know how long I was down below. It could have been days."

"Ned, Charlie, take Jem back to the *Sea Wolf*," ordered Captain Blade. "Give him something to eat. He looks half starved."

"You don't want to trust him, Captain," said Peter, as Jem was helped over the planks to their ship. "You only have to look at his eyes. I reckon he went mad and killed the others. I've heard as how the food on the *Truro* would drive anyone to madness."

Sam had to stifle a laugh. He didn't think anyone could produce worse meals than Peter.

"It's you who's going mad, Peter," declared Ben. "One man against a whole crew?"

"Aye," piped up Fernando. "Where's the blood?"

"And how did he make those holes in the hull?" added Harry Hopp. "And spill all that ink?"

"There's no treasure in the hold," said Fernando. "So either the monster took it or he's lying about that too."

"I believe his tale's true," said Blade, firmly. He looked round the stricken ship. "There's nothing more we can do here. The *Truro* won't stay afloat for much longer, I'll warrant. We'll get underway. That creature from hell could be lurking somewhere below, so we must put as many miles as we can between the *Sea Wolf* and certain death."

"Aye," said Ben Hudson, rubbing his beard anxiously. "I've no wish to meet a giant octopus that eats men and treasure."

The crew jostled to be first along the wooden bridges back to their ship, their eyes shifting uneasily over the ocean. As soon as the planks had been heaved on board, Harry shouted the order.

"All hands on deck! Full sail to the west." He turned to the captain. "Let's make for Hispaniola. The nearer we are to land, the safer we'll be, by my reckoning."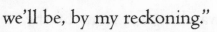

Blade nodded and took the wheel. "You're right, Harry. I don't want to be the monster's next meal — though part of me would like to go hunting for it!"

The crew shouted in protest.

"Settle down," said their captain with a

grim smile. "I'll not risk our lives for that beast."

"Shall I go back to the crow's nest?" Sam asked.

"No, lad," said Blade. "Give Ben a hand with the cannon. We need to be ready for action in case it appears again. Harry, station men along the rails to keep watch. The closer they are to the water, the quicker they'll spot the fiend."

Sam dashed up and down the steps to the gun deck, carrying kegs of powder to place next to each cannon. As soon as they were primed and ready, he ran to join Fernando and the crewmen, who were anxiously watching for signs of the creature. He looked out over the sea. The waves sparkled in the bright sunlight and the wind sent light clouds drifting across the blue sky. It seemed impossible that a sea monster could be lurking close by.

"I think we may be safe, my friend,"

Fernando told Sam. "Surely the beast would have attacked us by now."

"Aye," agreed Ned. "Perhaps one ship's crew was enough to fill its belly. It's probably long gone."

Sam couldn't help feeling disappointed. He could just picture the monster looming into view, rearing up for the attack and then cowering back at the sight of brave Captain Blade and his fearless band. The men of the *Sea Wolf* would banish it from the Caribbean!

Something caught his eye and he stifled a gasp. Was that a dark shape moving beneath the surface? He couldn't see anything now. It must have been the shadow of one of the clouds above.

Then, to his horror, the water below the bows began to bubble and heave. It looked as if the sea was boiling in a witch's cauldron. A huge weed-covered body burst through the waves, squirting jets of dark liquid across the deck. Massive arms swayed in the air. One, longer than the others, ended in a vicious claw like the pincer of a giant crab.

The claw towered menacingly over the *Sea Wolf*.

CHAPTER FOUR

Cold fingers of fear ran through Sam's body. He was face to face with a giant, man-eating octopus. Two of the creature's arms pounded the ship's side, making the *Sea Wolf* rock wildly. Overhead, the massive claw was slowly opening. Sam could see the white faces of his shipmates staring in terror at the hideous sight. Sinbad, the ship's cat, raised his hackles

and howled, ready for a fight.

"Fire!" yelled Captain Blade. "Loose the port cannon."

For a moment it looked as if no one was going to obey. The crew seemed frozen to the spot.

"Fire, I say!" thundered Blade. "Unless you want to be swallowed up!"

The pirates leapt into action, setting fuses to all the cannon.

BOOM! The deafening sound thundered across the deck. The cannonballs hit the water close to the monster's body, sending spray high into the air. The claw made a snap at the sails before the creature shrank back and began to sink below the waves.

"Full sail," ordered Blade. "We'll get away while we can."

This time the crew were quick to obey.

"Heave to!" shouted Harry, as the crew tugged at the sheets — the ropes that controlled the sails. "Put your backs into it."

"We're doing our best," cried Charlie, "but nothing's happening."

Harry threw a quick glance upwards. "Mainsail's flapping loose!" he yelled. Sam could hear the fear in his voice. "That cursed fiend must have torn it from its fixings."

"Then we'll not give it the chance to do more damage," said Captain Blade fiercely, his powerful arms heaving at the wheel. "Unfurl all topsails. That will give us some speed. Sam and Fernando, go and repair the damage as quick as you can."

"Aye, aye, Captain."

Sam slung a length of rope over his shoulder and followed Fernando in a desperate scramble up the rigging. He could feel the *Sea Wolf* lurch beneath him as the crew worked to bring her round and make their getaway. The sails flapped and the sheets creaked in their pulleys. As they reached the mainsail they could see it hanging loose from its wooden yard.

"It's a powerful beast," said Fernando, edging out onto the yard. "If it comes back before we've got all sails working, I fear we'll meet the same fate as the *Truro*."

Sam looked down. The water was calm now. *Somewhere under there it could be waiting for us*, he thought with a shiver.

"Perhaps we've scared it off," he said aloud, trying to sound hopeful.

Fernando muttered something in Spanish. Sam couldn't understand the words, but he knew that his friend was as frightened as he was.

"Pass the rope!" called Fernando. "I'll do a quick repair, but it will need more work when we have time."

If we ever have time, thought Sam before he could stop himself. He knew he mustn't think like this. He saw Captain Blade at the wheel below, calmly giving his men orders. If he could be brave, then so could Sam.

He crawled out towards Fernando with the rope. Then he lay flat on the yard, passed Fernando one end and hauled the loose sail up. Fernando began to thread the end of the rope through the holes in the sail.

"All shipshape?" came a squawk and Crow landed next to Sam.

"No, it's not," grunted Sam, holding on tightly to Fernando's rope. Crow peered at him for a moment then scuttled off to the other end of the yard where he began chomping at the wood.

The boys worked on in silence, dragging at the heavy, flapping cloth. It was almost ripped from their fingers by the gusting wind, but at last Fernando managed to tie the rope in a firm knot. He sat on the yard and punched the air.

"Success!" he whooped. "Give me one of your high fives!"

Sam held up his palm. "OK," he said with a grin, "but not too hard. Last time you nearly knocked me overboard!"

The boys smacked their hands together.

"Mainsail secure, Captain!" Sam shouted.

At that moment, the ship lurched violently.

"What was that?" cried Sam. But he already knew. The hideous monster was back! Its arms were thrashing against the *Sea Wolf*'s hull again, rocking her from side to side. The giant claw loomed over the deck as if searching for prey. Then it began to rise, tearing through the mainsail as if it was paper.

"Look out!" cried Fernando. "It's after us!"

"Make for the crow's nest!" yelled Sam.

He scrambled desperately up the rigging. Behind him, Fernando gave a sudden shout of terror. Sam turned to see the giant claw clamping itself like a vice round his friend!

Fernando was clutching at the mast with all his strength, but the creature was too powerful. Before Sam could get to him, the claw had torn him away.

"No!" shouted Sam. He couldn't let his friend be devoured by the monster. As the claw swung past he leapt at it and clung to the scaly pincers, trying desperately to force them open.

"It's no good," gasped Fernando, pinned tight inside the claw. "Jump while you've got the chance."

"No way!" panted Sam. "I'm not giving up."

The sea and sky whirled past Sam's eyes as the claw whipped him through the air. Then it stopped with a sickening jolt. Sam looked down. He wished he hadn't.

The monster's gaping mouth lay waiting below. Inside he could see a cavernous throat and the glow of a fiery belly.

Suddenly the claw opened and both boys were falling, arms and legs fighting the air. Horrified, Sam closed his eyes. Any second now he and Fernando were going to be eaten alive!

CHAPTER FIVE

Sam and Fernando tumbled through the air into the hungry jaws. They landed with a jolt. Sam opened his eyes and gasped in astonishment. This was no monster! They weren't in a fiery belly. They'd fallen into a large cabin, lit by swinging lanterns. Sam's brain whirled as he tried to take in the strange surroundings. The air was hot and smelled terrible — even worse than the boys' changing room after football practice. In front of them was a high platform like a foredeck. On it stood a ship's wheel with a brass octopus entwined around its spokes. Beyond that was a weird control panel, full of levers and handles, each one decorated with bright golden octopuses. Above it all rose a large window. Shoals of fish were flitting past the thick glass.

"We're under the sea!" gasped Fernando.

It's a submarine, thought Sam in amazement. Through the window he could see his ship's retreating hull.

Sam realised that Captain Blade and the crew had seen him and Fernando swallowed up by a monster. They probably thought the boys were dead and, at this very moment, were sailing away as fast as they could so they didn't share the same fate. There was no hope of a rescue.

Two pairs of strong, burly arms pulled them to their feet. Sam stared up into the scarred face of a brutish-looking man.

"Don't try anything," he snarled in Sam's ear.

A third man appeared at the top of the platform steps. This one was small and weedy with a pale, pinched face and eyes that darted about. He wore a braided coat and a captain's hat, with the brim curled up in front as if to make him look taller. All his clothes were too big for him.

"Nice of you to — heh, heh — drop in," he said in a thin, whining voice. "Welcome to the *Octopode*, my incredible underwater craft."

"Craft?" said Fernando, bewildered. "But it ate us!"

Fernando's captor, an ugly thug with a shaven head, gave a sneering laugh.

"This isn't a monster," Sam quickly told his friend. "It's a machine that can travel under the sea."

"How is that possible?" spluttered Fernando.

"I see you're impressed!" said the little
man. "And everyone else will be too when
they hear of this fantastical beast. The
name Septimus Grind – that's me – will
be famous throughout the Caribbean . . ."

He flung his arms out dramatically. "And, soon, throughout the world! Thanks to this glorious invention I will gather treasure where I choose. Nothing can stop me. I'll build a whole *fleet* of *Octopodes*. No ship will be safe in the Caribbean. I will be the richest and most famous pirate that ever lived."

"You're mad!" cried Fernando, struggling to free himself. But the shaven-headed guard held him in a vice-like grip.

"On the contrary, boy," said Septimus Grind. "I am a genius! You are witnessing modern piracy at its best. This is 1706 after all, not the dark ages! Why depend on the fickle wind to fill your sails when you can move unseen below the surface of the sea?"

"But where's the engine?" asked Sam before he could stop himself. "I mean . . . how do you make your *Octopode* move through the water?"

"Why do you think I plucked you from the rigging?" said Septimus, evil delight on his face. "I need manpower, of course."

"But I can't see any oars," said Fernando, still looking dumbfounded. "And sails don't work under the sea."

"Oars?" scoffed Septimus. "Sails? Don't be so foolish. The *Octopode* is driven by propelling paddles. You can't see them from here. They're on the outside of the hull and powered by my amazing capstan here in the cabin. Show them, men."

The boys were forced round to look
at a stout metal post in the centre of the
deck. Six wooden bars stuck out from its
sides like spokes on a rimless wheel. A
man was shackled to each bar, held captive
by leather wrist straps. Two were slumped
over their bars and all of them looked half
dead with exhaustion.

"My amazing capstan is attached to
a complicated series of cogs and axles

under the deck," Septimus went on. "The axles are joined to the propelling paddles." He poked a bony finger at the captives. "When these lazy wretches turn the capstan, the paddles whirl round and my *Octopode* moves swiftly through the water." He let out a mad laugh. "It means that we can travel faster than any sailing ship."

"Don't forget the ink, Captain Grind," called Fernando's guard. "That's my favourite bit. It squirts out so that our victims think they've been attacked by a giant octopus."

"I was coming to that, Fry!" snapped Septimus. "Everything about my *Octopode* is incredible. My Adjustable Spying Pole, for example." His hand shot out to grasp the end of a long tube that hung down from the cabin roof and he stared intently into a small hole in its side. His sharp nose and glinting eyes reminded Sam of an evil bird of prey. "The top always

stays on the surface, no matter how deep we go. With a series of mirrors I can see my target. And it gives me a supply of lovely fresh air too." He let out a manic laugh. "Now, I know what you're thinking — ships will see the top — but no. It is cunningly disguised as an innocent seagull, bobbing merrily on the waves."

Wow, thought Sam. *He's invented a periscope.*

"And my *Octopode* is so efficient," Septimus went on, "that it only takes three men to keep it running smoothly. One genius — that's me — and two trusty crewmen, whom you've already met." His eyes narrowed and he stamped his foot. "But we're wasting time. Cratchett, put these boys to work."

"Aye, aye, Captain Grind," said Sam's guard.

Fry pushed Fernando aside and unbuckled the two slumped prisoners from the capstan. He dragged them across to a low grilled door in the side of the cabin, threw them into the dark cell  where other men lay and slammed the door shut with a clang. Chuckling to himself, he turned the key in the lock and hung it on a hook on the wall. Sam shuddered. The cell was no more than a cubbyhole. The prisoners couldn't even stand upright.

While Fry still had his back to them, Sam saw Fernando's hand moving stealthily to his belt. In one swift move, he had a knife up against Cratchett's throat.

"Let my friend go!" he cried.

CHAPTER SIX

C ratchett cursed and released his grip on Sam.

Fernando rounded on Fry, who was edging along the wall towards him. "Keep still," he threatened, "for I can throw this knife quicker than you can blink!"

Fry held up his hands.

Sam looked round quickly for an escape route. The only exit seemed to be the jaws they'd fallen through – and the jaws were on top of the Octopode. He just hoped the top was still above the surface. He spotted a rope ladder hooked against the wall. They could reach the opening from there.

"This way," he called to Fernando. A plan was forming in his head. "If we can get out quickly, our crew might still be close enough to see us and we'll be rescued."

"And if they're not, we'll swim to them!" said Fernando grimly.

He held his dagger in front of him as they backed towards the ladder. Sam pulled it loose. They scrambled towards the closed jaws. Reaching out from the ladder, they both heaved to open the metal teeth. Sam knew they didn't have long. Grind's henchmen would be after them any moment.

"The jaws won't move!" panted Fernando.

"Keep trying!" said Sam, gritting
his teeth with the effort, but he feared
Fernando was right.

"Ready to give up now, boys?" came
Septimus's whiny voice. He was standing
at his wheel, smiling smugly at them. "You
see, the jaws only open when I pull a lever
– and I'm certainly not going to do that
for you." He gave a little snigger. "Now
we've had our fun, it's time to get you
down and put you to work. Cratchett, Fry,
see to it."

"Anyone who puts a foot on the ladder will have this between the eyes!" growled Fernando, brandishing his dagger.

"It's no good, Fernando!" whispered Sam. "We've got to think of another way."

"I'll be 'aving that knife," snarled Fry, hauling Fernando down and wrenching it from his grasp. "No more tricks now." He pressed the point of the dagger into Fernando's back. "Or you'll find this between your ribs."

Sam and Fernando were dragged to the two empty places at the capstan. Fernando cursed as the leather straps were buckled tightly round his wrists. Sam was shackled to the bar behind his friend. He could feel the manacles almost stopping the blood to his fingers.

"Get these miserable men moving," screeched Septimus. "I want the paddles going at top speed! We're on the hunt again."

"You heard him," snarled Cratchett. He pulled a vicious whip from his belt and flicked it towards the capstan.

The six prisoners began to walk in a circle, pushing the bars of the capstan slowly round. Sweat poured from them as they strained in the stifling heat. Loud clanking noises rose from somewhere below the floor. Sam felt the *Octopode* surging forwards.

Cratchett and Fry stomped off to a large barrel near the back of the craft. They each took a tankard and filled them with water from a tap in the barrel's side. Sam could hear them gulping it down. They smacked their lips and raised their tankards in a mocking salute to the parched prisoners.

Septimus was grasping the wheel with his bony fingers, steering round a coral reef. Then he pushed the wheel away from him and Sam felt the *Octopode* dive deeper into the dark ocean.

It's like the joystick on my flight simulator game, he thought. *He can go in whatever direction he wants.*

"You won't get away with this," shouted Fernando.

"Oh, but I *am*," called Septimus over his shoulder. "And you lucky boys are helping to power my *Octopode* as it sneaks up on my prey."

"God help your next poor victims," said Fernando between gritted teeth.

"Who are you after this time?" demanded Sam boldly.

"The *Sea Wolf*, of course," said Septimus. "She got away and I don't like being beaten."

Sam saw Fernando's whole body stiffen with shock and felt red hot anger coursing through his own veins. "Our crew will be ready for you this time!" he shouted.

The two guards began to advance on him, fists clenched.

"Leave him be!" snapped Septimus. "If you hurt him, he can't work."

Grumbling, Cratchett and Fry went back to their tankards.

"You're no match for Blade and his men!" exclaimed Fernando.

"Don't you be too sure," said Septimus, rubbing his hands with glee. "I am going to sink your ship and all hands with it. You see, I have invented a scuttling tool that will cut through your ship like a hot knife through butter."

Sam gave a horrified gasp.

"I call it the Drill of Death!" hissed Septimus, a mad gleam in his eyes. "Your precious *Sea Wolf* is doomed!"

CHAPTER SEVEN

"You coward!" Fernando yelled at Septimus. "You're too scared to face the men of the *Sea Wolf* in a fair fight so you have to sneak up on them."

"Fair!" shrieked Septimus Grind. "Why should I be fair? No one's ever been fair to me. I wasn't allowed to join a pirate ship and yet I had so much to offer."

"You don't have to sink the *Sea Wolf*,"

Sam called as he trundled round, pushing the heavy capstan as slowly as possible in the hope that his ship would have time to escape. "There's a pile of treasure aboard her – and a crew of strong men." *A crew of strong men who could overpower you and your thugs*, he thought to himself. "You'll be rich," he went on, "and you'll have plenty of slaves to power your *Octopode*."

Septimus turned and gave Sam a piercing look. He seemed to be considering the idea.

"And you'll never find better men than Captain Blade and his brave buccaneers anywhere in the Caribbean," added Sam.

"I *am* a bit short of slaves," said Septimus thoughtfully. Then his brow furrowed. "But it's Blade we're talking of here! I will have my revenge on him and his cannon no matter how much treasure is on board. There are plenty more vessels out there from which I can gather slaves and treasure." He grasped his wheel again.

"The *Sea Wolf* must be destroyed."

"Good try, lad," came a weary voice behind Sam. "But you'll get no sense out of that madman. We're all doomed."

Sam twisted round to peer over his shoulder at the man who had spoken. He wore a coat like Captain Blade's but it was tattered and torn. His beard showed dark against his white face and his manacled wrists were covered in bleeding blisters.

"Captain Trebennick's right," panted the prisoner opposite Sam. "We're going to die here."

"Are you from the *Truro*?" asked Fernando.

The man nodded. "I'm the first mate. George Lydgate's the name."

"It feels as if we've been here forever," said the captain weakly. "We won't survive much longer. We've had little food or water and it's hard to breathe in this foul place. The life's being sucked out of us."

George Lydgate's bloodshot eyes held a look of defeat. "That toad, Grind, doesn't care. He gets plenty to eat and drink, *and* the best of the fresh air from that spying device of his."

"Keep your voice down," warned Trebennick, casting an anxious glance at the henchmen. "If those two thugs of his catch us talking there'll be hell to pay."

"We found your ship," Sam told them in a low voice. "Jem Plunkett was the one man still on board."

"Then many of our crew have perished,"

said the captain sorrowfully, "for there's just the ten of us here."

"Ten against that weed Grind and his henchmen," said Fernando. "Couldn't you have fought them off once you arrived here?"

"Not in the state we were in, lad," said George. "We were plucked half-drowned from the sea in ones and twos. By the time we knew what had happened, those brutes had seized us and shackled us to this infernal machine – or thrown us in that cubbyhole of a brig."

"Curse Grind's weaselly eyes!" growled Captain Trebennick. "I remember him from years ago when I was a rigger on my first ship. He came strutting aboard, telling us how he was going to be the best pirate ever."

"And was he?" asked Fernando.

Trebennick gave a hoarse laugh that turned into a rattling cough. "He didn't

know port from starboard," he wheezed.
"He was scared of heights and he got
seasick — and all before we'd left harbour.
He was flung off the ship. The crew were
glad to see him go. He had mad ideas even
then."

"And now he's going to
destroy the *Sea Wolf*," said
Sam. "We've got to
stop him."

He dug his
heels into the floor
and pulled with all his
strength, determined
to stop the capstan
from turning
and propelling the
Octopode towards his
ship. But Cratchett had spotted what he
was doing. He flung down his tankard.

"I can see your game!" he bellowed,
raising the whip.

Sam tensed, waiting for the stinging blow across his back.

There was a deafening squawk and a flash of green shot across the cabin towards Cratchett. Sam couldn't believe his eyes. It was Crow! He must have flown in when they were captured and been hiding ever since.

Septimus was gripping the foredeck rail, his eyes narrowed in fury. "Catch that bird!" he snapped.

"Enemy below!" screeched the parrot, digging his claws into Cratchett's hand. The henchman cursed, dropped the whip and made a grab for him. The bound men brought the capstan to a halt, hardly able to keep from smiling.

"Rough seas!" shrieked Crow, circling

away and flapping into the air for another
onslaught.

"Well done, Crow!" whooped Fernando.
"You can beat him!"

As the furious parrot dived at Cratchett,
Sam suddenly caught sight of Fry creeping
up, holding a sack at the ready. "Look
out!" he yelled.

"Awkkk!"

It was too late. The shaven-headed guard
had thrown the sack over the parrot and
was holding it tightly shut. Sam could hear
Crow's angry, muffled cries.

"Let him go," pleaded Sam in
desperation. "He's harmless."

"Harmless?" growled Cratchett,
snatching the sack from Fry. "Dangerous,
more like." He pulled Crow out, gripping
him tightly in one enormous hand. Crow's
eyes bulged as he struggled to get free.

"Kill it!" screeched Septimus. "Do it
now!"

"There, my pretty," said Cratchett, rubbing a rough finger over the green feathers. "Stay still for me. It won't hurt much when I wring your neck!"

CHAPTER EIGHT

"**N**o!" yelled Sam, straining at his shackles. "You can't kill Crow!"

Cratchett stopped and looked at him in surprise, the parrot dangling from his fist.

Septimus Grind fixed Sam with a fiery gaze. "You're not the one giving the orders around here, miserable prisoner," he barked. "*I* am the one with the power of life and death over you all, and *I* say the parrot dies!"

"You'll be sorry!" shouted Fernando.

"And why is that, pray?" asked Septimus coldly. "Speak, or Cratchett will wring your neck too!"

"Because . . . because . . ." faltered Fernando.

"Because this parrot is a very rare breed," said Sam, thinking quickly. "We couldn't do without him on the *Sea Wolf*. He can tell you if your enemies are nearby and take messages and . . . and . . . he can smell treasure from twenty leagues away!"

"Pieces of eight!" squawked Crow in a strangled voice.

Septimus looked hard at him. "Hmm," he said at last. "That could be very useful. I have decided. The parrot can live. But if he lets me down, I'll wring his neck myself!"

"He won't," Sam assured him. "He's very reliable."

"Lock the bird away until I need him, Cratchett," ordered Septimus.

The henchman curled his lip in disgust, dropped Crow into a wicker basket and fastened the lid shut.

"Just remember, you're all at my mercy," said Septimus. "Anyone who steps out of line will pay a heavy price." He suddenly realised that the *Octopode* wasn't moving. "What are you gawping at, you lazy lot? Cratchett, get them working. The *Sea Wolf* must not escape my clutches this time."

Cratchett snatched up the whip from the floor and flicked it round the feet of the six captives.

Already Sam could feel his back and shoulder muscles aching as he pushed his capstan bar. The men of the *Truro* had been working like this for days. Surely they couldn't survive much longer in this hot stale air. After five minutes he felt he could hardly breathe! And the harder they pushed, the nearer they were coming to Septimus's target — the *Sea Wolf*. He had to do something.

He glanced over at the two henchmen, who now stood together glaring at their captives.

"If only the guards weren't looking at us all the time," Sam muttered to Fernando, "we'd have the chance to free ourselves."

"And then?" panted Fernando.

"The cell key's hanging on the wall," said Sam in a low voice. "We could get it and release the others."

Fernando nodded. "Agreed, and between us we could overpower Septimus Grind and his men and take control. The question is, *how* do we get free?"

"There must be a way," said Sam through gritted teeth. *Captain Blade wouldn't give up*, he thought to himself, *so neither will we*. But he knew there was nothing they could do while the guards were watching.

He plodded round behind Fernando, risking a glance towards the giant window. There was no sign of the *Sea Wolf* yet, only the waves rippling the surface above and sea creatures darting away from the strange craft.

Maybe she's sailed away to safety, Sam thought desperately. *Septimus can't go on looking for ever.*

A shark flashed past the window and, as it went out of sight, Sam spotted a familiar

dark shape in the distance. In spite of the hot, clammy work, a cold feeling began to creep over him. It was the hull of his ship.

The *Octopode*'s captain was looking eagerly through his periscope. He swung round towards them and did a little jig on the spot. "The *Sea Wolf* is in view!" he shrieked. "I can see her flag. She's ahead to port – or is it starboard? It's of no matter. Wherever she is, I'm not letting her out of my sight."

He moved the wheel and the *Octopode* slowly changed course. Now it was making straight for the doomed vessel. Cratchett and Fry hurried to the foredeck steps and gazed eagerly up at the window.

"She doesn't stand a chance, Captain Grind," chuckled Cratchett.

Septimus had his eye at the periscope again. "Such a shame," he sniggered. "The *Sea Wolf* is a sitting duck. She's got no wind and we have underwater power!"

Sam tugged helplessly at his leather

manacles, fear stabbing at him. "Got to get these off!" he muttered. "Got to save the ship!"

Fernando suddenly slumped over his post. His head began jerking from side to side. For a moment Sam thought with alarm that his friend was ill. Then he realised what he was doing. He was opening one of the buckles of the manacles with his teeth!

Great idea, thought Sam. He bent over, determined to do the same.

"Oi!" came a shout. Cratchett and Fry were marching over to Fernando. Cratchett seized two of the capstan bars to bring it to a halt.

Sam froze.

"What's going on?" called Septimus angrily.

"Trying to get yourself free, were you?" growled Cratchett. "Well, let me help you!" He unbuckled Fernando from his manacles and held him up by the scruff of his neck.

"What shall I do with him, Captain?"

Septimus's eyes flashed with pure venom. Sam felt as if his heart had stopped beating. What terrible punishment would this madman come up with?

"Throw him in the brig," ordered Grind savagely. "He can't do any harm there. I'll deal with him later. And get another man to take his place. We haven't got time to waste."

Fernando kicked out, catching Cratchett on the shin. The brute gave a yelp of pain, staggered backwards and crashed into Fry.

The two guards sprawled on the floor in a heap. Fernando took his chance. He grabbed the key from the wall and made a dive for the cell door.

"Go, Fernando!" called Sam. His friend was going to free the prisoners before their captors could get to their feet!

"Do something!" shrieked Septimus.

Just as Fernando turned the key in the lock, Cratchett's hand came down hard on his arm. "I'll have that!" he growled.

Fernando was bundled into the cell and another prisoner hauled out to be strapped to the capstan in his place. Sam could see his friend, crouching down, squashed in the tiny brig with the other prisoners.

"Cratchett, give me the key!" shouted Septimus. "It'll be safer with me."

The guard took the key to his master. As he passed the capstan he cracked the whip in the air. "Get moving!" he bellowed.

Sam and the others began to trudge

round again. Sam felt the sweat trickling into his eyes. He longed to rub them with his fists but had to make do with wiping his forehead on his sleeve. He knew that now he was the only one who could stop the *Octopode* from attacking the *Sea Wolf*. Cratchett was with Septimus, and Fry was making a great fuss, rolling around on the floor clutching his belly as if he was almost dead. He looked like a footballer faking an injury in front of the ref. But that didn't help Sam. Fry would give up soon — well before Sam had managed to free himself. He had to come up with something else but he was too exhausted to think straight.

And time was running out. Captain Blade and his crew had no idea what deadly danger lurked beneath the waves.

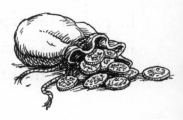

CHAPTER NINE

There was a sudden scratching on
the floor by his feet and Sam stifled
a cry as something sharp dug into his
jeans. What new horror was this? He
peeked down. Crow was climbing up
his leg, a determined look in his beady
eyes.

"How did you escape?" Sam whispered.
The parrot pulled himself onto the bar,

and spat out a shred of wicker. "Clever boy," Sam told him. "You've chewed your way out of the basket! But you're in danger if you stay here."

He knew Cratchett would be back to watch over them at any minute. And Fry was on his feet again. Grind's henchmen couldn't help but spot Crow's bright green feathers.

Crow had begun to attack one of Sam's manacles with his beak. Sam nudged at

him urgently with his nose. "Go and hide before you get your neck wrung."

But the parrot wasn't giving up. He took one look at his enemy and swung down under the bar. Sam could feel him gnawing on the leather manacle, hidden from the henchman's view. Although every muscle in his body was throbbing with pain, Sam's hopes began to rise. If Crow could chew up a starboard rail and two chair legs, he'd have no trouble with a leather strap. Sam didn't know what he was going to do once he was free, but he was determined to think of some way of getting the key from Septimus. With all the prisoners freed, it would be twelve against three and he didn't think Captain Grind would be much of a fighter.

The *Sea Wolf* was coming nearer and nearer. Soon its hull hung in front of them, filling the whole view.

"Come on, Crow!" muttered Sam, feeling the manacle loosen slightly. "You're our only hope now."

"We're in the perfect place!" cried Septimus jubilantly. "Stop the paddles."

"Halt!" Cratchett bellowed at the captives working the capstan.

The men flopped over their bars, panting with exhaustion.

"And now for the grapples to secure us to the ship," shrieked Septimus, seizing a lever in each hand.

Sam saw two of the octopus arms suddenly shoot out from above the window and embed their claws in the *Sea Wolf*'s hull. They were acting like clamps to keep the *Octopode* steady.

"Poor old Captain Blade," cackled the mad scientist. "You're not going to get away from me this time!"

Sam tugged at the gnawed manacle. He could almost get his hand out. "That's it,

Crow!" he murmured. "A few more bites and I'll be free."

"Cratchett, Fry, get the Drill of Death into position." Septimus waved at his henchmen. "I want both of you to turn the crank. I'm not trusting those pathetic slaves with this important job."

"Aye, aye, Captain Grind," growled Cratchett. "Blade and his men will be in Davy Jones' Locker before they realise what's happened!" He stuck the whip in his belt and climbed up to the foredeck. Fry followed. Together they began to turn a wooden handle, their muscles bulging with the effort. A deep cranking noise rumbled through the *Octopode* and a giant metal drill slowly appeared in the water between the grapples, relentlessly making its way towards the hull of the

Sea Wolf. This was Sam's chance — no one was looking at him. The three men were too busy with the drill.

Sam gritted his teeth and yanked his hand back as hard as he could. This time he could feel it slipping out of the manacle. At last, it was free!

"Thank you, Crow!" Sam whispered. "Now, hide — quickly!" But the parrot gave him a determined look and went on gnawing at the other manacle. In desperation, Sam grabbed Crow and stuffed him up the back of his jerkin.

"Kidnapped!" protested Crow in a muffled voice.

Sam felt him squirming about and then heard a steady chomping. The parrot had found his belt. At least that would keep him busy for a while. Sam began to undo his other manacle.

"That's it, shipmate," whispered George Lydgate. "You're nearly there."

Now Sam had both hands free. He caught a glimpse of Fernando's anxious face through the brig door. His friend was gripping the metal and his knuckles were white. Sam cast a glance at Cratchett and Fry. The henchmen were still concentrating on the drill handle, groaning with the effort. But the end of the drill had reached the wooden hull. Sam had to hurry. He was about to creep under the bar to get to George when a shrill voice rang across the cabin.

"What are you doing, boy?" Septimus was glaring at him.

Sam quickly thrust his hands back into the open manacles.

"I want you scum ready for work!" Septimus snapped at the cowering prisoners. "As soon as we've scuttled the ship, we're off, so it doesn't drag us down, too."

Sam felt his knees going weak with relief. Septimus hadn't seen that he was free. But his ship was in terrible danger.

Septimus had a look of evil triumph on his face. "And now, a show for you miserable wretches," he announced, flinging his arms wide. "The sinking of the *Sea Wolf*! And there's nothing anyone can do about it. Goodbye, Captain Blade!"

CHAPTER TEN

The *Octopode* gave a shudder as the drill began to bite into the *Sea Wolf's* timbers.

"Faster," Septimus shrieked at his henchmen, who panted as they strained to turn the crank. He whirled round to stare eagerly through the window. "I want to see the water pouring into that hull. Blade will not escape me twice."

Sam knew he had to take his chance while Septimus had his back to him. Ducking low, he swiftly unbuckled Captain Trebennick's shackles, then released the others. They looked exhausted but couldn't hide the sudden hope on their faces.

Sam had to think quickly. The six of them might be more than a match for the puny Septimus Grind but, after the gruelling work and lack of food, the men of the *Truro* would have a hard fight against Grind's brawny henchmen. Sam quickly scanned the cabin. There was nothing they could use as weapons. They'd have to take the villains by surprise. He signalled for the men to make for the steps.

Fernando was watching silently. He mimed a high five at Sam.

"We'll split up and take one brute each," ordered Captain Trebennick in a low voice. "Three to each man should do it. We can deal with that little squirt afterwards."

"Miserable sprat!" came a muffled squawk from Crow. Sam could feel him under his jerkin, clinging to his belt. He hoped the parrot had the sense to stay there.

Septimus's hands were spread over the window and his nose was pressed to the glass, like a toddler gazing into a sweetshop. "Soon that vessel will be at the bottom of the sea and every man drowned. Turn that lever harder. I want to see the drill cutting into the wood."

No one had noticed the prisoners creeping up the stairs. Sam's heart was beating painfully hard. Time was running out. A few more turns of the drill and water would start gushing into the *Sea Wolf*.

Captain Trebennick led his group towards Fry. Sam and the others made for Cratchett. As the brute began to straighten, ready for another turn of the crank, Sam tapped him on the back. The henchman spun round, gave a gasp of surprise and swung a punch at him. Sam ducked and the force of the swing sent Cratchett tumbling over Sam to land with a thump on the planks of the foredeck. Sam could hear Fry cursing as his three attackers held him and bound him with their bandanas.

Septimus cowered away in terror. "Help!" he shrieked. "Mutiny!"

Cratchett was struggling to his feet.

Sam leapt onto his back and clamped his
hands over his eyes. Cratchett thrashed
about blindly, clawing at Sam's fingers.
Now Sam's team joined in, punching and
kicking furiously. With a bellow of rage,
the guard shook Sam off, flinging him
down the steps to the hard deck below.
Crow flapped out from Sam's jerkin with a
frightened squawk.

Sam lay there, trying to catch his breath. He could see that Cratchett had pulled his whip from his belt and was lashing at his attackers. The two men backed away to avoid the painful stings.

"Well done, Cratchett," squeaked Septimus. He grasped the crank and tried to turn it. "Now, keep them away while I finish the job."

"That won't be a problem," snarled Cratchett, letting the whip swish round the floor. "They'll not venture near the cat-o'-nine-tails!"

Suddenly the air was full of ear-splitting squawks. Crow hadn't forgotten being half throttled! He was coming for his revenge. Cratchett dropped the whip and drew a knife from his belt.

The five *Truro* men began edging towards him. Sam leapt up to join them.

But Cratchett was slashing the air with his knife, keeping his attackers at bay. Crow gave a screech and flapped away to cling to the periscope. No one could get near the vicious guard. Then Sam spotted the whip lying on the ground. He threw himself down as if in terror of the knife, waited for his moment and snatched it up. He had no idea how to use it but it couldn't be that hard. He'd seen it in films loads of times – the hero always managed to pull the villain's gun or knife from his hand with a whip. He tried to give it a crack with a flick of his wrist but his palm was damp with sweat and the whip just curled feebly in the air.

Cratchett laughed. "You silly, weak boy!" he snarled. "You can't get the better of me."

He raised his knife over his head and lunged at Sam. In terror, Sam lashed out. As Cratchett gave a cry of triumph, the leather thongs caught round his knees. Sam jerked the whip hard and Cratchett crashed to the deck next to Fry, his legs bound together.

Before he could move, the men of the *Truro* had him trussed up with his own belt and neckerchief. Fernando and the prisoners in the brig gave a cheer. Sam

pulled the whip free and advanced on Septimus, who was cowering behind the wheel.

"Mr Grind," called Sam, flicking the cat-o'-nine-tails with a satisfying crack. He was getting the hang of it now. "Your men are a bit tied up, so *we're* giving the orders."

"It's Captain Grind to you," hissed Septimus defiantly, "and no one gives me orders."

"I think you'll listen to us," said Sam. He cracked the whip again. Septimus let out a squeal of fear. "The first thing you will do is get that drill out of my ship's hull."

"But it hasn't cut through yet," wailed Septimus. "Just another couple of turns . . ." He looked round at the grim faces of the men advancing on him and sighed. "Very well," he said at last, "I will do as you say. I have no choice."

"We can't trust him," snarled George Lydgate. He pushed Septimus aside and cranked the handle in the opposite direction.

To Sam's huge relief, the drill began to slide back towards the *Octopode*. The *Sea Wolf*'s timbers were splintered but there was no hole.

"Now, make those grapples release the *Sea Wolf*," Sam demanded.

Without a word, Septimus pulled on the levers. They all saw the arms unclamp and felt the underwater craft float free.

"Step away from the wheel," ordered Captain Trebennick.

"As you wish," said Septimus meekly.

Sam was struggling to keep the grin from his face. He'd saved the *Sea Wolf*! Now all he had to do was set the prisoners in the brig free and get this weird submarine up to the surface. Septimus had slumped over his controls, his cheek resting on the

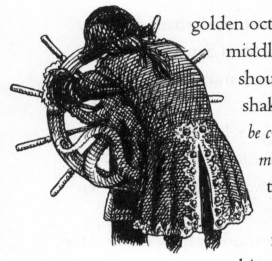

golden octopus in the middle. His shoulders were shaking. *He must be crying over his miserable defeat,* thought Sam. He almost felt sorry for him.

But then he realised with a jolt that the man wasn't crying – he was laughing!

With a wild shriek of delight, Septimus threw back his head and seized the golden octopus in both hands. Before Sam could stop him, he twisted it violently round.

At once, Sam heard the ominous sound of rushing water.

CHAPTER ELEVEN

"Surely you didn't expect me to give in that easily," shrieked Septimus. "I have just set in motion my dreaded Dial of Doom."

Slits had appeared in the walls of the *Octopode* and water was beginning to stream down into the cabin.

"One twist of my wonderful dial and the *Octopode* has opened its gills to let in the ocean!" sniggered the mad inventor. "It won't be long before you all drown!"

The water was creeping across the lower deck.

Sam pushed Septimus aside and tried to twist the golden octopus back. It didn't move.

"Don't bother," the mad inventor told him. "I've designed it to work one way only. It's very simple. The *Octopode* will fill and then it will sink." He opened a hatch at his feet. Sam glimpsed a small barrel-shaped craft in a chamber under the foredeck. "I have my escape pod ready," Septimus told him with glee. "It's already loaded with my treasure."

"But I won't let you go!" said Sam desperately. "Get us up to the surface and open the hatch."

He held the whip ready to strike and stood between Grind and the escape hatch.

A cunning look came over Septimus's face. "The lower deck is filling up fast and the brig has a very low ceiling," he told Sam. 'Even if I do as you say, your incarcerated friends will have drowned long before we reach the surface."

"Then give me the key to the prison," demanded Sam.

Septimus took it from his belt and looked at it thoughtfully. "Let me go and it's yours. It's your only chance to rescue your friends. If you try to take it from me, I will drop it down into my hatch and you'll never get it."

Sam knew there was no time to argue. The men in the brig were calling desperately for help.

"Agreed," he said, reaching out to take the key.

Quick as a flash, Septimus threw it over Sam's head. Sam tried to catch it but it disappeared into the steadily rising water on the deck below.

He hurtled down the steps after it and heard the hatch close behind him. The villain had got away, but Sam didn't have time to worry about that! He had to find the key and release the others before they perished.

He dropped onto all fours to search. It was too dark to see anything and the only thing he could feel was the rough wood of the floor.

Captain Trebennick and his crew came bounding down the foredeck steps and waded across to help. The water swirled about their knees. Sam caught sight of Fernando's anxious face at the bars. It wouldn't be long before the little cell was completely engulfed.

"Treasure hunt!" squawked Crow, fluttering above Sam's head.

"Come on, my friend!" shouted Fernando. "You can do it."

"We've got to be quick!" cried George. "This craft is sinking fast with the extra weight of the water in here."

"But there's no sign of the key," Sam said desperately. He swept his hands round in wide arcs. But his fingers felt nothing. "Keep calm!" he muttered to himself. "It's here somewhere."

He crawled further along. Suddenly he let out a yelp as he knelt on something hard. His fingers curled round it. It was the key!

Sam jumped to his feet, splashed over to the cell door and unlocked it. Fernando burst out of his cramped prison and raced up to the foredeck, making straight for Fry.

"I'll be having this," he said grimly as he took his knife back.

"Man the capstan," cried Sam, scrambling up the steps after Fernando. "We've got to make for the surface." He pulled the wheel towards him as he'd seen Septimus do. *Thank goodness he'd reached level twenty-seven of Flight Simulator. His mother always moaned that he spent too long on that game. Little did she know how useful it had turned out to be!* The *Octopode* slowly tilted. Sam steered the vessel up beside the *Sea Wolf's* hull.

Fernando joined the ten men from the *Truro* as they took hold of the capstan bars and began to push. The water was up to their waists now.

"We can hardly move it!" shouted Fernando.

"The craft's heavier with that flood coming in through the gills," said Captain Trebennick. "We need more power."

Fernando nodded at the henchmen lying

bound on the foredeck. "I say we untie them."

"Aye," puffed George Lydgate. "They're strong and they've not been slaving like us. We know that to our cost."

"Can we trust them, though?" asked one of his shipmates.

"We'll do whatever you say," gabbled Cratchett. "Just don't let us drown."

Fernando sliced through their bonds. The henchmen threw themselves onto the capstan and the craft began to move.

Sam held the wheel steady. "We're nearly there," he called. "Keep going."

But the water seemed to be rising faster now.

Sam could see Fernando struggling to keep his head above the surface. He wanted to dive

down and rescue him but he knew they'd all be lost if he stopped steering.

"We're going to die," whimpered Fry.

Sam gave a sudden shout. "I can see daylight!"

As the *Octopode* broke through the waves, the snarling wolf figurehead of the *Sea Wolf* came into view.

Captain Trebennick held Cratchett's knife to his throat. "How do we open the jaws of this thing?"

Cratchett nodded fearfully towards the foredeck. "The boy can do it. The lever's on the side of the wheel."

Sam seized the lever and pulled. With a grinding clunk, the jaws of the hatch began to open.

The *Truro* men abandoned the capstan and swam frantically to the rope ladder that hung down from the hatch, eager to climb up and squeeze through the slowly widening gap. Yelping with fear, Cratchett and Fry splashed after them. George Lydgate led the way as they scrambled up to the opening. He had just reached the top when something whistled past his head and struck the body of the *Octopode*, sending splinters flying. Everyone tumbled back down the ladder in terror.

Sam's hand froze on the lever.

"They think we're the monster," he yelled. "They're shooting at us!"

CHAPTER TWELVE

"I'll show myself," declared Fernando. "They won't fire on a shipmate."

Captain Trebennick looked up. The *Octopode* was being peppered with shot. "You'll be dead before they realise who you are."

"We'll be dead if we stay here," said George Lydgate.

"We've got no choice," insisted

Fernando. "We're just lucky we're too close for them to use the cannon. Get those jaws wide open, Sam."

There was a determined squawk and, suddenly, Crow flew past Fernando and zoomed out of the *Octopode*. "Abandon ship!" he shrieked.

"Hold your fire!" came a distant shout. "That's Crow. Who else be still alive in that beast? Friend or foe?"

"Friend!" yelled Fernando, climbing out

onto the top of the *Octopode* and waving frantically. "Sam's here, too, and there are others. We're all very glad to see you."

"They're alive!" came Charlie's cry.

"And that's how we wish to stay," called Captain Trebennick, ushering his men up the ladder.

Sam wanted to whoop with joy. Everyone was safe! There was just him to go now. He was about to swim over to the escape ladder when a movement through the window caught his eye. Something was feebly splashing around. Had one of the *Truro* men fallen into the sea? He seized the periscope and peered into the small eyehole. A little barrel-shaped craft with two spindly arms was paddling around in circles not far from the *Octopode*. It was Septimus in his escape pod! Apparently, he couldn't steer it. Sam wasn't going to let him escape again.

Fernando poked his head down through

the jaws. "Come on," he called. "Time to go."

"I'll be there in a minute," Sam replied. "I've got one last job to do here."

"Be quick!" Fernando sounded anxious. "The *Octopode*'s sinking again. The sea will be coming in through the hatch soon."

Sam knew he didn't have long. The water below had now reached the foredeck. It was lapping over his feet. He grabbed the levers that operated the giant claw — the claw that had plucked him and Fernando off the *Sea Wolf*. He realised that they worked like the game on the pier at Backwater Bay where you operated a crane to win a toy. This claw was much harder to manoeuvre, but finally he got it swinging across the surface of the ocean towards Septimus's barrel. He opened the claw and positioned it above the mini *Octopode*.

The weaselly inventor had no idea what was looming over him.

"You're about to get a taste of your own medicine," Sam muttered through gritted teeth.

The claw slammed down around the barrel. Sam pulled on the lever and raised it out of the sea, but time was running out. He could feel the cold water rising up his legs.

"Sam!" Fernando's cry was urgent. "You must leave now."

Sam began to swing his catch over to the *Sea Wolf*. He was going to deliver Septimus neatly onto the deck. The barrel was almost over the rail when a small door opened in its side. Arms waving like a windmill, Septimus went tumbling into the sea.

"No!" yelled Sam.

A shudder ran through the *Octopode*, throwing Sam to the floor. He looked up to see water gushing down through the open jaws. Septimus's monster was sinking and it was taking him with it! He plunged off the foredeck into the swirling currents, fighting to get to the ladder. At last he had it in his grasp. He pulled himself onto it, bending his head against the force of the cascading torrent. It was all he could do not to be washed away. He thrust his hand up to the next rung, and the next. He could do this! Blinded by the deluge, he had no idea how near he was to the hatch, but it couldn't be far away now.

But no matter how fast he climbed, the water was rising faster. It reached his chest, now his neck. He sucked in a deep breath as he was engulfed in the dark, salty flood. He yanked hard on the rope ladder and, to his horror, he felt it go loose in his hands.

It had broken away.

He tried to kick up towards the jaws but the *Octopode* lurched suddenly and he felt himself turning over and over. He had completely lost his bearings.

Sam thrashed about in the water, trying to get to the opening. His chest was hurting as his lungs cried out for air. He was good at holding his breath, but up until now it had always been a game in the swimming pool in Backwater Bay. This was deadly serious. If he didn't find the hatch soon, he'd drown.

Something knocked against his shoulder. Sam reached out and touched a human foot. He recoiled in horror. There was a dead body right next to him! Cold hands were grabbing at his jerkin. Was this a nightmare? Had he gone to Davy Jones' Locker, where skeletal pirates preyed on drowned bodies? He fought himself free. He felt the hands clutching at him again. Now they had him under the arms. They seemed to be pulling him down through the swirling ocean to the depths of the sea bed. There was nothing he could do. He closed his eyes. His whole body was aching and he knew he couldn't last much longer without oxygen. He'd have to take a breath and, as soon as he did, his lungs would fill with water.

He was going to die.

CHAPTER THIRTEEN

S am took a huge gulping breath. He waited for the cold water to rush into his lungs. Instead he felt clean fresh air surge into his body. He could hear men shouting and seagulls screeching overhead. He opened his eyes and found himself staring at Fernando. That had been no skeleton attack — his friend had dived back into the *Octopode* and saved his life!

Now they were floating on the surface and above them rose the massive hull of the *Sea Wolf*.

"I've got him!" Fernando yelled to the watching crew. "Haul us up."

Before he knew what was happening, Sam found himself on the deck, surrounded by his cheering shipmates. Crow flapped down onto his head and Charlie flung her arms round his neck.

"Well done, Sam!" she exclaimed. "The men of the *Truro* told us what you did as soon as they came aboard. You're a hero."

She backed off, grinning. "A very wet hero!"

"Fernando's a hero, too," said Sam. "I'd have drowned if it hadn't been for him."

"Well, as you couldn't bear to leave the *Octopode*, I thought I'd better drag you out," laughed Fernando, untying the rescue rope from around his waist. "I dived down and plucked you up. It would have been a lot easier if you hadn't put up such a fight, though."

"We never thought to see either of you again after you were swallowed up by that monster," said Ben.

"And it wasn't a monster, after all," said Charlie, her eyes wide. "Captain Trebennick's been telling us all about Septimus Grind's fiendish underwater contraption and what he planned to do to us."

"Aye," said Ned. "We felt something

strike the ship but we had no notion it was something so deadly as a drill. You saved us from being scuppered."

"Give 'em a medal!" squawked Crow.

"We're proud of you both, lads!" said Harry Hopp, patting them on the back.

"And me and my crew are grateful," agreed Captain Trebennick. "We owe you our lives."

"Anyone would have done the same," murmured Sam. He felt as if his brain had been washed away and seaweed left in its place, but something was niggling at him. He was sure he had some unfinished business.

"Septimus!" he cried suddenly. "I tried to catch him with the *Octopode*'s claw but I think he got away."

"Oh, no, he didn't!" came a deep voice.

The crowd parted and Sam could see Captain Blade, one hand holding a heavy

sack and the other clasping the bedraggled
figure of Septimus Grind. Septimus still
had his hat on. It was rammed firmly onto

his head. "The fool nearly drowned. He wouldn't let go of his treasure."

Sam punched the air in delight. "But how—" he began.

"Simple," said Charlie. "We saw the little sprat flapping about in the sea and fished him out."

"Didn't seem fair to leave the poor thing to the mercy of the sharks," added Ben with a grin.

"Us pirates are all heart!" said Ned.

"What about his men?" asked Sam. "Did they get rescued?"

"Aye, lad," said Harry Hopp, jerking a thumb over his shoulder. "And they're under the fiercest guard we've got."

Cratchett and Fry were huddled together under the mainmast. Sinbad, the ship's cat, sat staring at them, flexing his claws.

"They won't be moving in a hurry," laughed Charlie.

"Never mind them!" Septimus stamped

his foot. "Unhand me this instant! I am the great Septimus Grind! Do you not recognise me?"

Blade scratched his head. "Can't say that I do," he said calmly. "But, by the stars, I recognise a scoundrel when I see one."

"Scoundrel?" squeaked Septimus. "I am no scoundrel. I am the greatest inventor the world has ever known! My name shall live for ever."

You're wrong there, thought Sam. *No one's heard of you in the twenty-first century.*

"You think you've beaten me, you ignorant fools," Septimus ranted on, "but you have not. I will make my escape, be sure of that, and I will build a whole fleet of *Octopodes*. The Caribbean will be mine! And, after that, the world . . ."

"Well, stick my sardines in a saucepan," laughed Ned, "the man's as mad as a March hare."

Septimus was pulling at his damp jacket.

"I have the construction plans hidden in here!" He frantically searched his pockets. "Where are they?" he yelped. "Who has stolen them from me?"

Sam peered over the side of the ship. Pieces of paper were slowly bobbing away on the waves. "Do you mean *those* construction plans?" he asked helpfully.

Septimus looked out over the sea. "My plans!" he wailed. Then, as he watched the ocean rise and fall, his face went green. "Seasick!" he groaned, clapping his hand to his mouth.

Peter whipped Septimus's hat off and held it out for him just in time.

Meanwhile, Blade emptied the contents of the sack onto the deck. Everyone gasped in admiration at the silver goblets, gold coins and sparkling jewels.

Harry Hopp rubbed his hands. "We've got a good haul here, Captain."

"Aye," said Blade, "but it's not ours to keep."

There was a muttering amongst the *Sea Wolf* men.

"Why not?" protested Ben. "You're not going to give it back to that madman, are you?"

"Grind took it from the *Truro*," Captain Blade told the crew. "Usually it's finders keepers, but today there are men here who fought bravely – and they have greater need of it than we do."

"There's more than enough there to buy our new ship," said Trebennick. "I insist we share it between the two crews by way of thanks."

Blade nodded and the captains solemnly shook hands.

"We'll put you ashore in Port Royal," said Harry Hopp. "There's many a good vessel to be bought there."

"What of Grind and his men?" asked George Lydgate. "What will their punishment be? They deserve to walk the plank."

Trebennick turned to his first mate. "We can have a think about that," he said. "I'm tempted to keep the scoundrels on our crew. Cratchett and Fry are strong and I can't think of a worse punishment for that landlubber, Grind, than making him suffer from seasickness all his days. And if he ever manages to cope with the life, he can invent ways to make our new ship go like the wind."

"I'll warrant he'll not be inventing anything like his octopus contraption again," said Harry Hopp. "Making a craft that goes under the water – the man is indeed mad!"

"Aye to that," chorused the crew.

Sam hid his smile. He couldn't tell them that in his time there were submarines all over the ocean. His shipmates would think *he* was mad.

"Set sail for Port Royal," ordered Blade. "Ben, break out the rum. We'll have a tot to celebrate."

Sam suddenly felt a tingling in his fingers and toes. He knew what that meant. He was about to return to the future. He was sorry to leave his friends but he didn't mind missing the rum. It tasted like toilet cleaner and one sip made him feel as if his head was going to explode.

With a secret wave to Charlie, he ducked down out of sight so that no one would see him disappear. He felt himself being sucked into the familiar dark tunnel and deposited back in his bedroom, dripping salt water all over his carpet. He looked down at his jeans and T-shirt. His mum would not be pleased if she could see the state they were in now. He didn't think she'd believe him if he said he'd accidentally fallen in the bath! He tore them off and went to stuff them under his bed. Then he remembered his doubloon. He wasn't going to leave it in his pocket and risk losing it in the washing machine again! He took it out and stowed it safely back in the old bottle.

Now he could be sure of going back to the *Sea Wolf* and all his friends for another amazing pirate adventure.

CREW MANIFEST

Sinbad

Crow

Thomas Blade
Captain

Peter Craddock
Ship's Cook

Fernando
Rigger

Don't miss the next exciting adventure in the
Sam Silver: Undercover Pirate series

DEAD MAN'S HAND

Available in December 2013!
Read on for a special preview
of the first chapters.

CHAPTER ONE

Sam Silver clung to the rigging of the
Sea Wolf. He could hear the frightened
shouts of his crewmates below. The
blinding rain lashed down and a vicious
wind ripped his clothes. Sam looked out
at the churning sea. Wave after wave
was breaking over the ship's rail, sending
foam far into the air and making the ship
lurch dangerously. Suddenly a wall of

grey water blocked everything from his
view. It towered over him, higher than the
tallest mast. The crew cried out in terror
and, with a horrific cracking sound, the
ship smashed in two. Before Sam knew
what was happening he was torn from
the rigging by the force of the water and
found himself tumbling headlong into the
sea. Down, down he fell, sinking through
the swirling ocean, struggling helplessly to
push his way back to the surface. He was
going to drown . . . he needed air . . . he
had to take a breath . . .

Sam woke with a start, gulping hard. He

sat up and looked round wildly. He could breathe! He wasn't at the bottom of the ocean. He was in his own bedroom. The *Sea Wolf* hadn't sunk and his pirate friends weren't lost after all. It had all been a horrible dream.

But what if his nightmare had been a warning of some kind? He'd been on board the ship in many storms and he knew how dangerous they could be. He needed to know if Captain Blade and the crew were safe – and he couldn't phone them. There was only one way to find out. Sam turned on his light, took down the dirty old bottle that he kept on his shelf and tipped out the precious gold doubloon inside.

No one else knew the secret of Sam's gold coin. It had the power to whisk him back three hundred years in time to join Captain Blade and his bold crew on board the *Sea Wolf* – the best pirate ship that had ever sailed the Caribbean Sea.

Sam hastily threw on the old jeans, T-shirt and trainers that he always wore when he went pirating. He spat on the coin and rubbed it on his sleeve.

At once his tangled sheets, his pillow and his crumpled pyjamas whizzed around him as if he'd been caught in a giant vacuum cleaner. He closed his eyes and felt himself being lifted into the air. In the next instant, he landed in a heap on something hard. He opened his eyes quickly and found he was in the ship's storeroom that he knew so well. The floor was rocking gently. He couldn't hear any crashing waves or howling wind. The *Sea Wolf* hadn't been sunk.

But the horror of the dream was still lingering in his head. The ship might seem fine but he had to make sure that all his shipmates were OK. He ran over to a barrel where a pirate jerkin, neckerchief, belt and spyglass lay waiting for him. His friend Charlie always put them there, ready for his return. She was the only girl on the crew and the only one who knew he came from the twenty-first century. He couldn't tell the rest of the crew. They'd think he was mad.

Sam ran out of the storeroom and bounded up the steps towards the deck. Just before he reached the top, he stopped, dazzled by the bright sunlight. The sails billowed against the blue sky as the wind sent the ship scudding across the waves. Happy voices reached his ears and Sinbad the surly ship's cat was asleep on a coil of rope. He opened one evil eye and hissed at Sam. Sam crept past, giving him a wide berth. Sinbad was the fiercest member of the crew and nobody could go near him except for Charlie. If Sinbad was being his usual self then everything must be all right.

Sam jumped down onto the main deck
where the pirates were crouched round
sacks and chests piled high on the wooden
boards. Captain Blade was standing in the
middle of his men. He wore red braids in
his beard and two belts full of fearsome
weapons across his chest.

"By the heavens, it's Sam Silver!" he
boomed as Sam ran towards him.

The pirates got to their feet, grinning. A boy, his wild curly hair tied in a bandana, leapt on Sam and gave him a hearty punch on the arm.

"My frrriend!" he exclaimed in delight. Fernando's Spanish accent always got stronger when he was excited.

Ned the bosun gazed out over the empty sea, looking puzzled. "Well I'll be a barracuda in a basket," he said. "How did you get here, Sam? There's no vessel in sight and I'm certain you didn't swim."

"Maybe he was dropped by an albatross!" laughed Ben Hudson.

Sam's brain buzzed as he tried to think of a way he could have reached the *Sea Wolf*. They wouldn't be laughing if he told them the truth!

"He must have stowed away on a passing ship," said Charlie, coming to his rescue as usual.

"Charlie's right," Sam added quickly. "It

was . . . a fishing boat. And you can't see her now because she's gone. When the *Sea Wolf* came into sight I jumped overboard in a barrel, paddled hard and here I am!"

"You're a true Silver!" declared the captain. "Your grandfather would have been proud of your wily ways."

All the crew but Charlie believed that Sam was the grandson of Joseph Silver, a heroic pirate, long-since dead. Sam went along with this. It was almost true. Joseph Silver had been his great-great-lots-of-greats-grandad, and it was Joseph's gold doubloon that brought Sam back to 1706. When Sam went home to the present, they all believed that he'd gone to help his poor widowed mother on her farm.

"Sam has Silver's luck too," said Ben.

"Aye, and a pirate's nose," agreed Harry Hopp, the first mate. "He can smell a treasure haul from a hundred miles!" He led Sam to the pile of sacks and chests, his

wooden leg thumping on the deck.
"You're just in time to help us sort our
plunder!"

working leg down on the deck.

Come, put it in to help me swim a stroke painted...

CHAPTER TWO

"Brilliant," said Sam. "Where did the treasure come from?"

"We took it from the *Master of the Ocean*," said Captain Blade. "Titus Reynard's ship."

"Who's he?" asked Sam.

Oops, he thought at once. *The crew are all looking at me. This is someone I'm meant to know.*

"Sorry, I must have seaweed in my ears," he

said, giving them a rub. "Who did you say again?"

"You know Titus Reynard, Sam," said Charlie, fixing him with her eyes. "The rich merchant from Puerto Rico. He took over all that land on the eastern tip of the island and built the grandest house you ever saw. You must have heard of him. He's the biggest villain around these parts."

"Of course I have," said Sam nodding vigorously. "Big villain, lots of land. Who hasn't heard of him?"

"I wish Titus had been on board when we attacked," said Ben. "I'd have enjoyed seeing that cur watch his treasure disappear!"

"Luckily that lily-livered brother of his was there to entertain us," laughed Ned. "He kept leaping about and shouting, though none of his men took any notice."

"I warrant his crew would've fought

harder if Titus had been on board himself," said Captain Blade. "All his servants live in fear of him."

"Servants?" spat Peter the ship's cook. "Slaves more like, the way he treats them."

"Aye, none last long under his harsh rule," agreed Ned.

"Didn't they even try to follow you to get his treasure back?" asked Sam in surprise.

Fernando fingered the blade of his knife. "We told them what would happen to them if they did!"

"And we slashed their sails – just in case they changed their minds," added Charlie.

"Belay this talk!" ordered the captain. "Get the booty out for all to see."

"Pieces of eight!" came a loud squawk and a green parrot landed on Sam's head.

"Hello, Crow," Sam said in delight, coaxing him down onto his shoulder. He began to open one of the sacks while the parrot chattered in his ear.

Captain Blade gulped and backed away to the rail.

The *Sea Wolf* captain could face the most fearsome sea monster and not turn a hair but the sight of Sam's feathery friend had him quivering in his shoes. Peter the cook said it was because a parrot had poked its beak up his nose when he was a baby, but all the crew had a different story to tell.

Since Blade so disliked parrots, everyone just pretended that Crow was a brightly coloured Caribbean crow. It was the only way that Blade would let him stay on board.

The crew dived on the sacks and chests, cutting them open and thrusting their hands inside to pull out the treasure.

"Well, boil my brains in a bucket!" exclaimed Ned, throwing a cheap metal goblet to the deck. "There's nothing of worth here!"

"Aye," agreed Harry Hopp, holding up a string of gaudy beads. "These are just glass."

"Perhaps that's where his wealth comes from," called Captain Blade. "He buys rubbish but tricks people into paying a lot for it."

"Yet Reynard's brother was shouting about 'the last piece of the puzzle' and 'the key to untold wealth'," said Charlie in surprise, "and he said he had to get it to Titus or his life wouldn't be worth living."

Fernando shrugged. "Just words to try to make the crew obey him. There's no key here . . ."

". . . and not enough wealth to buy more than a tot of rum in a tavern!" said Ben in disgust.

"Search again, men!" ordered Blade. "We might have missed something."

Muttering, the pirates began to pick gloomily through the piles of tin plates and cheap jewellery. Sam found a dirty wooden box under a sack. "Maybe there's something in here," he said hopefully. "No one's opened it yet."

"Having seen the rest of the cargo, it'll probably be someone's false teeth!" laughed Fernando.

Sam threw open the lid. Inside was a lumpy shape wrapped in an oilcloth. As he picked it up, the cloth fell away. Sam leapt back in alarm.

Something fell from his hands and clattered to the deck. It was a skeletal hand.